Happ...

GW00357484

Switch I.T. Off!

CONSTABLE

How **not** to use this Paper Smartphone

Unlike ordinary smartphones and tablets, touching this Paper Smartphone's screen will not change the image or alter what you see in any way.

Go on. Try it now. Nothing happens. See?

You can, however, change what you see by drawing on this screen if you like.

Go on. Try that too. Draw something on this page now. Make it yours.

How **to** use this Paper Smartphone

Switch I.T. Off! is designed to be
dipped into, leafed through, passed around, coloured
in, scribbled on, and even ripped up.

It's all about having fun, any way you want, either
on your own or with your friends. We've tried to
pack it as full as possible with games, illusions,
jokes, puzzles, crafts, tricks, and other activities and
challenges that will both inspire and entertain.

We hope it gets people talking, face to face.
And laughing, together.

To **switch it on**, all you need to do is
turn the page and then start flicking through…

in-phone search engine

To help you find what you're looking for inside *Switch It Off!* we've included these handy little icons which will tell you what to expect…

let's go outside

we prefer it in

tricksy pixiez

arty farty

dares & challenges

kind of dumb

pithy quotes, facts & stats

spam

face book

Draw your face on this page

Show it to someone else and ask them if they know who you've just drawn

phombies

Hidden in this Paper Smartphone are six phombies (phone zombies) – all not looking where they're going.

Tick in the magnifying glass when you find them.

get lost!

Who knows where life will take you next?

Be spontaneous and go somewhere unexpected.

From where you are right now, either in your car or on foot (with a responsible adult, of course):

→ take a right turn

→ take the next left

→ and the right after that

→ the next left

→ the next two rights

→ another left

→ go the nearest café

→ ask directions to the closest green space or park

→ sit in the park and look at the clouds

help Gary now!

Yikes! Poor Gary has lost his mobile phone and is having a total and utter meltdown! Can you help him find it before he starts to cry?

edible
zombie makeover

That's right, the time has come to turn yourself into a zombie using only edible household ingredients such as:

guacamole   **jam**
mushy peas   **ketchup**
honey   **cereal**
flour   **marshmallows**

The only rule you now need is this:

"Use the goo to apply the dry!"

Now get zombifying. YOU are ground zero.

Let the Apocalypse begin.

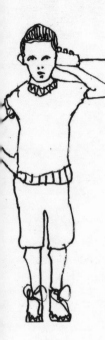

smartphone

Everyone thinks mobile phones are some kind of new-fangled invention, well here's the proof that they're not.

Anyone can make a phone – and not just a paper one either – we're talking homemade phones that really, truly work!

What you'll need: string, 2 plastic cups, 2 paper clips, scissors, or a sharpened pencil for poking holes

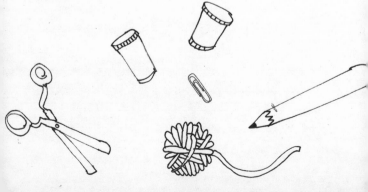

LIKE IT'S 1979!

What you'll need to do:

- cut a six-foot length of string
- poke a hole in the bottom of each cup
- push the ends of the string through the holes into the cups
- attach the ends of the string to the paper clips, so they can't be pulled back through
- high fives all round, your Fone79™ is now ready to use
- get a friend to hold one end, while you hold the other
- move away from each other until the string is tight
- take turns, with one of you talking into their cup, while the other one listens
- have fun chatting and also raise a smile at how small your monthly bill will be*

* to enable your Fone79™ with email, simply write messages on the wings of paper aeroplanes and throw them at each other while you chat

digitally emojify yourself!

What do you think these two finger folk are talking about?

Write what you think they're saying inside the speech bubbles.

Make your own finger folk too.

Draw their expressions with pens.

Give them a story.

Get other people to guess just what it is that's going on inside their tiny, meaty, boney heads.

autobiographise
me!

We're all worthy of having our own autobiographies in the shops. Who wouldn't want to know about all the incredible things that we've done?

But we'd need a good title, to really nail down who we are and what we're about.

Find a funny, or insightful phrase that sums up your life and could be used as the title of your autobiography.

Discuss with family and friends.

Examples of a few people we know:

"Treading on toys" – Kev

"Walking down hills in flip flops" – Helen

"What I saved on lunch, I spent on shades" – Lesley

dot com

Join the dots to see how joyful handsfree life can be.

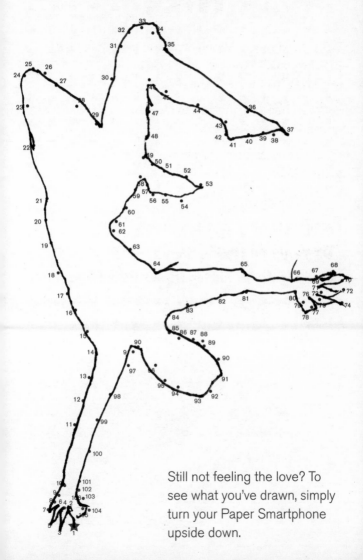

Still not feeling the love? To see what you've drawn, simply turn your Paper Smartphone upside down.

word up

a	k	r	b	h	s	t	r	e	l	a	w	q	u	t
d	r	a	n	t	i	s	o	c	i	a	l	g	h	w
h	x	o	t	e	d	l	a	t	i	g	i	d	x	e
c	h	q	g	a	g	c	y	t	v	l	y	w	g	n
e	j	x	t	g	x	b	d	r	k	w	d	e	q	t
n	n	a	d	d	i	c	t	i	o	n	h	m	q	y
o	p	g	z	s	c	n	f	e	h	p	w	a	m	f
h	h	q	k	e	p	s	t	r	e	s	s	i	j	o
p	u	a	i	b	o	h	p	o	m	o	n	l	p	u
t	b	o	y	s	o	g	m	l	p	g	h	n	d	r
r	b	k	r	y	k	e	m	f	h	o	o	e	s	s
a	i	j	l	s	l	e	v	d	c	p	w	e	p	e
m	n	a	i	n	m	o	s	n	i	e	x	o	a	v
s	g	k	x	y	t	e	i	x	n	a	k	y	m	e
b	v	g	l	j	s	t	e	e	w	t	p	e	a	n

digitaldetox	tweet
phubbing	stress
nomophobia	twentyfourseven
smartphone	insomnia
anxiety	email
alerts	antisocial
addiction	spam

"MEMORY IS A LOST ART. THESE DAYS WE RELY ON OUR PHONES, TABLETS AND COMPUTERS TO MEMORISE THINGS, AS A RESULT WE ARE NOT EXERCISING OUR MOST IMPORTANT MENTAL MUSCLE — OUR BRAINS."

Tony Buzan, Founder of the World Memory Championships.

Quote taken from 'How Croydon Will Host the World Memory Championships 2013' by Liz Sheppard-Jones in *The Croydon Citizen*, November 2013.

something fishy

Did you know that the collective noun for goldfish is a 'troubling'?

And did you also know that humans now have shorter attention spans than goldfish, thanks in large part to our digital lifestyles?

The average human attention span has fallen from 12 seconds in 2000 to 8 seconds today.

Goldfish have an attention span of 9 seconds.

It probably took you about 9 seconds to read this page up to here.

Did you manage to concentrate the whole time?

Can you remember the collective noun for goldfish?

Or should we maybe be asking a goldfish instead?

make your own screensaver

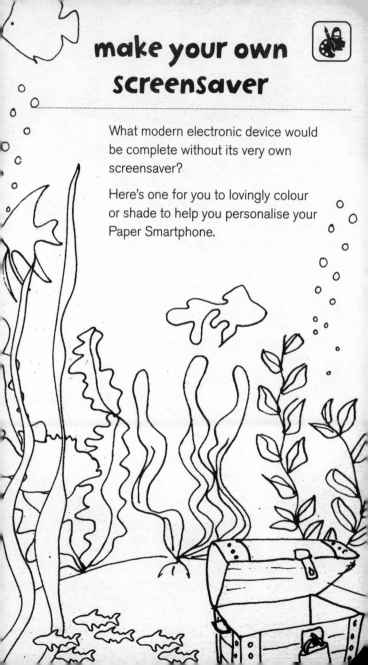

What modern electronic device would be complete without its very own screensaver?

Here's one for you to lovingly colour or shade to help you personalise your Paper Smartphone.

sun/day roast

A solar oven harnesses direct sunlight to heat or pasteurise food or drink. It's the ultimate green, fuel-free way to cook.

Here's how to make your own:

- Put a saucepan-sized cardboard box inside a slightly larger cardboard box and then insulate the gaps in between with shredded newspaper

- Line the bottom of the small box with black paper or paint it black (to absorb heat) and line its walls with tin foil (to reflect heat onto the food)

- Cover the inside of the four flaps of the big box with tinfoil, so that they'll reflect sunlight into the box when positioned almost vertically

- When you're cooking, and there's a pot inside the box, make sure to then cover the open top of the box with either a glass lid, or cling film (to let the sunshine in)

☀ Food cooks best in dark, shallow, thin metal pots. Tight-fitting lids keep in moisture and heat

☀ Sunlight is the fuel you're going to be cooking with, so make sure to position your oven somewhere that will be sunny for several hours, is protected from strong wind, and will be safe from predators

☀ Capture extra sunlight by using other shiny surfaces to reflect more light onto the pot, but be careful the light you're reflecting won't accidentally start any fires

What to cook? You can cook pretty much anything that will fit inside. People have even cooked their Christmas turkeys in big solar ovens!

nice slice, anyone?

Making bread is not only soulful and therapeutic, it tastes great too.

Here's how to do it:

1. You'll need 1kg strong bread flour, 625ml warmish water, 37g sachets of dried yeast or 30g fresh yeast, 2 tablespoons sugar, 1 level tablespoon fine sea salt and flour for dusting.

2. Wash your hands, don your apron and, on a clean surface, tip out all the flour and make a big mound. Now put your finger in and form a hole in the middle of your mound and spread it out so you've got a well.

3. Pour in half the water, then add the yeast, sugar and salt and stir.

4. Bit by bit get flour from the outside of your mound and carefully add it into the water in the well, continuously stirring it in with a fork until it gets all gloopy. Then add all the remaining water and finally incorporate the rest of the flour.

5. Now comes the really fun bit. Roll up your sleeves and get kneading. Push and punch your dough for 4 or 5 minutes, until you have a pliable, elastic dough.

6. Sprinkle flour on the top and put it in a large bowl. Cover with cling film and leave in a warm, dry place for half an hour until it has doubled in size – or proved.

7. Now bash the air out of it for 10 seconds and shape it into the loaf shape you require. Be creative. Leave it alone for another 30 minutes until it has doubled in size again.

8. Meanwhile heat the oven to 180 degrees/350F/gas4.

9. Put your loaf on a floured baking tray and gently push it into the oven. Bake for 25 minutes.

10. Take your masterpiece out of the oven and knock the bottom of your loaf. If it sounds hollow, it's done.

daytime cloud spotter

No, not that cloud, the one where we're all so busy storing all of our really, really important stuff and from which we're downloading all of our other really, really important stuff... we mean the clouds, the ones that give us water, and have been around forever, and will still be here long after we're all gone.

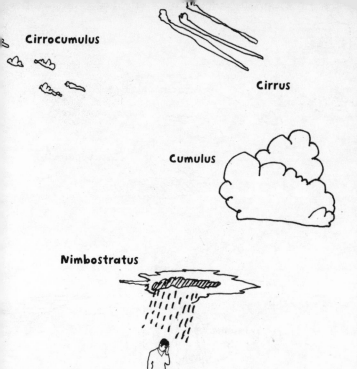

Clouds are made of water and even ice crystals higher up. They're categorised by how they look and how high up they are and there are ten basic types.

Why don't you look out of the window or head outside and see which ones you can identify?

Or perhaps you can find some new ones, ones that don't look like any of these at all, but instead look like other things, like dogs, rabbits, polar bears and whales...

Why not write down the ones that you can see, or even try drawing some here?

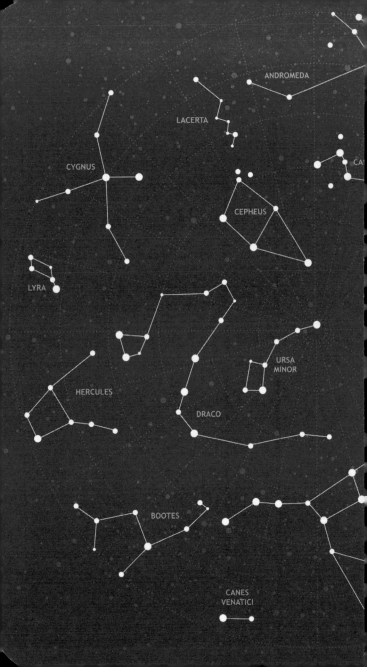

nighttime star gazer

A star is an object in the sky that sends out its own light and other radiant energy generated by nuclear reactions, much like our own sun.

Our own galaxy, the Milky Way, is home to around 300 billion stars and it's estimated that the observable universe has more than 100 billion galaxies.

Galileo first studied the night sky with a telescope 400 years ago. But there's plenty you can still see using only your eyes. Here are some famous formations to look for.

Tips:

★ Choose a clear night.

★ The less light pollution there is, the better you'll see, so try to find somewhere as far away from bright lights as possible. A back garden or even looking out of the window with the lights off will do. A field, a beach, or a park would be even better.

★ Be patient. It may take up to 20 minutes for your eyes to adapt to dim light.

★ Maybe sip a hot chocolate or put on some ambient or classical music to enjoy as you stare into deepest space and think your deepest thoughts.

How do you learn a poem by heart? Some people just recite them. Others write them down or type them, over and over until they're learnt, until they feel almost like they wrote them themselves.

Why do we learn poems by heart? Because they help us to feel. Because they make us smile, or sigh, or cry. Because memorising them means we can share them with somebody else.

Here are ten much-loved, well-known poems you might like to learn and then share.

in memorium

Try memorising this poem.

The Camel's hump is an ugly lump
Which well you may see at the Zoo;
But uglier yet is the hump we get
From having too little to do.

Kiddies and grown-ups too-oo-oo,
If we haven't enough to do-oo-oo,
We get the hump—
Cameelious hump—
The hump that is black and blue!

Rudyard Kipling

You could write it out here to help you remember –
or compose your own poem!

paper bottle opener

We've all been there. You're out camping, or down the beach, or sitting on a desert island after a shipwreck… you've got a great view and you've built up a thirst. But here's the thing. You've got plenty of bottled drinks with you, but nothing to open them with. So what are you going to do?

Simple. Use the nearest piece of paper to open those bottles up.

- All you need to do is fold that sheet of paper or card over and over until it's long and thin (about half the width of a bottle top).

- Now fold this length in half to make it even harder and stick the folded end under the bottle top and use your wrist to lever it up until it pops the top.

- You can even use cash if you're lucky enough to have some to hand. And paper napkins work too.

So there you have it. The perfect accessory for your Paper Smartphone. A paper bottle opener. Happy top popping.

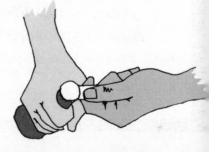

CHATROOM™

"New from Really Real Life Inc, the same folk who brought you the revolutionary Breathing™, Walking™ and Sleep™ apps which have enhanced so many lives, we now proudly present ChatRoom™!"

Revolutionary ChatRoom™ features include:

Wall™, for leaning against while your friends talk to you

Sofa™, for sitting on while you talk to your friends

Table™, perfect for resting snacks on to eat while you and your friends hang out

"Why delay? Revolutionise your social life today! Buy ChatRoom™ now!"

Warning. Unfortunately only real people, not people you just know online, can hang out here.

Disclaimer. Actual chat is not included in ChatRoom™. Customers will have to improvise this themselves.

tree-licious

Trees not only provide us with oxygen, wood and paper, they also give us a great excuse to head outside into the countryside or a nearby park.

Can you identify any of the trees below? Try and learn their shapes and their names.

Maybe climb one. Or sit under one and have a picnic.

Beech **Elder** **Weeping Willow** **Sweet Chestnut**

Or, if you end up feeling really at one with the world, maybe even give them a hug to thank them for everything they do for us.

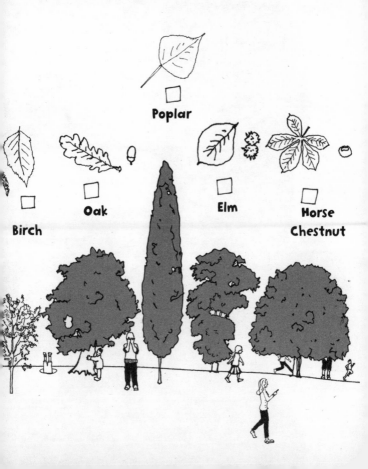

Poplar

Birch

Oak

Elm

Horse Chestnut

The average user now picks up their mobile device more than **1,500** times a week

The average user reaches for their phone at 07:31 in the morning

These users check personal emails and Facebook before they get out of bed

Average owners use their phone for 03h16 a day

Almost **4/10** users admitted to feeling lost without their device

(Source: Tecmark Survey 2014)

How often do **YOU** look at your phone per day?

Be honest.

Write down that number here:

Now write down the number you wish you looked at your phone instead and think about what you could be doing with that extra time:

Now make that wish come true.

phone alone

1. Confiscate your friend or relative's real phone

2. Hide it

3. See how long they can go without it

4. Rate their reaction. As time goes by, the longer they're without it, do they look more like this:

Or this:

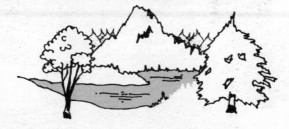

And what about you?

1. Did you prefer who they were with it or without it?

2. And what do they think about that?

dice me stupid

Switch I.T. Off!
and
GLUE

1.
trace the dice shape opposite onto a piece of card

2.
write an action word on each of the six sides of the dice, the sillier, the better, like: hide, burp, drink, tickle, hop, sing.

3.
cut out the dice shape on your card

4.
fold it and glue or tape its sides until you have a cube

5.
take turns rolling it with some friends

6.
take turns doing whatever the dice says – no hesitation or chickening out allowed!

tickle

drink

hop   hide   burp

sing

out loud

Say the following out loud:

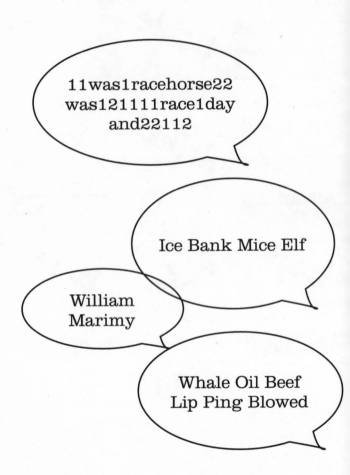

Snack attack!

So how terrific are your taste buds? Really?
We've all got a favourite flavour crisp, but can we
really tell them apart?

Especially when we've got a blindfold on…

What you'll need:

- crisps, and lots of them, several flavours at least
- pen and paper
- sticky tape
- bowls

a blindfold (test it out to make sure it really does work)

OK, let's go:

1. write down the names of each flavour crisp on a
small piece of paper

2. tape these to the bottom of several bowls

3. put the different flavoured crisps in the matching
bowls

4. shuffle round the bowls

5. let the taste test begin!

Make sure you keep score… this is a deadly serious
contest and test of wits, not merely a game…

this is not a rehearsal!

You, yes **YOU!**

What are you doing with your life?

Well, OK, obviously, right this very second, you're reading this, but we're talking about the rest of your life, your future, where you're going next, who you're going to be…

List six big ambitions for the rest of your life and set a deadline for each.

Make the first deadline soon.

MY **BIG** AMBITIONS:

		DATE TO BE COMPLETED BY:
1		
2		
3		
4		
5		
6		

'One look at an email can rob you of 15 minutes of focus. One call on your cell phone, one tweet, one instant message can destroy your schedule, forcing you to move meetings, or blow off really important things, like love, and friendship.'

Jacqueline Leo, Editor-in-Chief of *The Fiscal Times*.

Quote taken from 'Digital Dieting' in *The Huffington Post*, March 2010.

garage band

Be honest. Who out there hasn't at some point wanted to be in a band? But what would you call yourselves? How do you come up with a good name? Something original? Something that will really blow people's minds?

It sounds impossible, right? Wrong! Because thanks to the **RANDOM BAND NAME DICTIONARY GENERATOR™** it's now the easiest thing in the world.

All you need to do is:

- ♪ open a dictionary at a random page
- ♪ choose one word on that page
- ♪ try and match it with another word from another random page to form a really cool band name

Simple, huh? Now there's just the little matter of, er, oh yeah, learning how to play those instruments and writing those songs…

twist & shout

A tongue-twister is a phrase that's devilishly, deviously, difficult and overly-intricate to articulate.

Researchers at Massachusetts Institute of Technology (MIT) in Boston recently conducted a study where they asked people to repeat the phrase 'pad kid poured curd pulled cold' ten times in rapid succession. Many of the participants clammed up and stopped talking all together, they were so freaked out.

Here's our top ten tongue-torturing, mouth-mangling, throat-throttlers for you to try:

1 One smart fellow, he felt smart.
Two smart fellows, they felt smart.
Three smart fellows, they all felt smart.

2 Greek grapes, Greek grapes, Greek grapes

3 If Stu chews shoes, should Stu choose the shoes he chews?

4 I wish to wish the wish you wish to wish, but if you wish the wish the witch wishes, I won't wish the wish you wish to wish.

5 A big black bug bit a big black bear.
But where is the big black bear that the big black bug bit?

6 If two witches were watching two watches, which witch would watch which watch?

7 Rubber baby buggy bumpers

8 A skunk sat on a stump. The stump thunk the skunk stunk. The skunk thunk the stump stunk.

9 I slit a sheet, a sheet I slit, upon a slitted sheet I sit.

10 The winkle ship sank and the shrimp ship swam.

ugly bug

The term 'bug' was first used to describe a defect or glitch in a computer system in 1946 by Grace Hopper, when she traced an error in the Mark II computer at Harvard to a moth trapped in a relay. This moth is now part of the collection in the Smithsonian National Museum of American History.

We, the manufacturers of this Paper Smartphone have done everything in our power to remove all bugs from these pages.

We are, however, also aware that the threat of viral contamination is constant and we are therefore continuously cataloguing all new types of bug which may one day threaten the integrity of your Paper Smartphone.

To help us in our quest to hunt down all possible bug threats, please draw the oddest, ugliest bug you think might one day be invented here ·····································

Now give it a name. The more scientific-sounding the better, such as Uglyistus Bugzilla, or Shakitoffi Taylorswiftae. And write that down here.

··

··

Virus alert!

Your Paper Smartphone's Viradicator has detected a virus!
But fortunately this has now been removed!

To protect yourself from further viral attacks and hostile
hacking, we recommend you reset your password now.

Coming up with a good password that's hard to crack isn't
easy. But if you make it too complicated, you might not be
able to remember it.

Top tips for creating a great password you can remember include:

* Avoid single dictionary words, places and names.

* Keep it long. The longer your password is, the tougher it is to crack.

* Jumble it up and throw a few numbers into the mix.

Here's a step-by-step guide:

1. Write down a memorable phrase. Eg. "We love pizza!"

2. Write it backwards with a number in between each letter. Eg.
   "We love pizza!" would become: "!1a2z3z4i5p6e7v8o9l10e11W".

There. Hard to hack. But easy enough to work out if you ever
forget it too.

OK

'So, your kids must love the iPad?' I asked Mr. Jobs, trying to change the subject. The company's first tablet was just hitting the shelves. 'They haven't used it,' he told me. 'We limit how much technology our kids use at home.'

From 'Steve Jobs Was a Low-Tech Parent' by Nick Bilton, *The New York Times*, September 2014.

SPAM GLOVELOK™

Is someone in your life in need of a digital detox? Glovelok them today!

Glovelok's unique locking system can be programmed for up to 24 hours!

FORGET PLAYING GAMES!

NO MORE TYPING

STOP THEM TEXTING!

Warning. Glovelok™ may also interfere with other basic and essential human functions such as eating, drinking, and picking one's nose.

knowing me, knowing you

→ make up **five facts** about your life which are absolutely true and **one, plausible sounding lie**.

→ write them down below.

→ ask your family or friends to vote on which is true and which is a lie. You'll be amazed at what both you and they will discover.

Fact 1.

Fact 2.

Fact 3.

Fact 4.

Fact 5.

Fact 6.

shaken, not stirred

Ever dreamt of being a Mixologist? Well here's your chance, with our "Cheeky Custom Cocktail Challenge"...

You've got to not only invent your own cocktail, but name it too.

We're talking non-alcoholic mocktails for kids, and then either with or without alcohol for adults.

And while you're drinking it? Silly glasses, straws and accessories are an absolute must. Tuxedos are, of course, optional, but are highly recommended too.

Kids' example:
the "**Kiwi-Wee-Wee**": Blend 3 cups of crushed ice, 2 tablespoons of pineapple juice and 2 peeled and sliced kiwis. Chill in the fridge for half an hour and serve.

Adult example:
the "**Pratberry**": one part Noilly Prat vermouth, mixed with one part vodka, and three parts pureed blueberries. Serve with plenty of ice.

Most children play outside for less than an hour a day, a third of the time their grandparents did. 9 out of 10 children have never used a map or compass, played conkers, dammed a stream, or explored a cave.

Statistics from research commissioned by the National Trust as part of their 50 Things To Do Before You're 11 ¾ campaign, 2014.

top of the gargles

Gargling and serious music have always walked hand in hand, or at least simultaneously tapped their toes.

George Harrison of The Beatles favoured warming up by gargling a mix of honey, vinegar and warm water, a trick recommended to him by both Eric Clapton and Barbara Streisand. Indian film score composer R D Burman has featured gargling in his work. Joe Cocker's vocals are often described as 'gravel-gargling' – in a good way, of course.

Well, here's your chance to make a little rock 'n' roll gargle history of your own.

Grab yourself some liquid refreshment.

Think of a song.

gargle it

Get whoever you're with to guess what you're gargling.

Then let them take a turn.

Top Three Gargle Songs/Singers:

- Lady Gargle
- Radio Gargle
- Octopus's Gargle

What is this life if, full of care,
We have no time to stand and stare.
No time to stand beneath the boughs
And stare as long as sheep or cows.
No time to see, when woods we pass,
Where squirrels hide their nuts in grass.
No time to see, in broad daylight,
Streams full of stars, like skies at night.
No time to turn at Beauty's glance,
And watch her feet, how they can dance.
No time to wait till her mouth can
Enrich that smile her eyes began.
A poor life this if, full of care,
We have no time to stand and stare.

W. H. Davies

wake up & smell the roses

The smell of
fresh flowers is, of course,
sublime. Go and stick your nose
in a rose and breathe in.
Heavenly, right?

So why not bottle it and make your own
perfume?

Here's how:

- Pick or buy some roses, lily-of-the-valley, jasmine
  or honeysuckle.

- Pluck the petals and chop them so they look
  like confetti.

- Put them in a jar and cover with perfumer's alcohol
  (or if you don't have that, vodka will do).
  Screw on the lid tightly.

- Put the jar in a dark cupboard for 12 weeks.

- Strain the petals through a sieve.

- Pour the sieved liquid into a
  perfume jar and… voila!
  Your very own
  perfume.

weirdly
weightless arms

Stand in a doorway and press the backs of your hands onto the frame either side of you, with your fingers pointing down.

Really push…

As hard as you can…

For a whole minute…

Now step out of the doorway…

Wow… it feels weird…

Your arms are weightless and rising up…

As if they have a life of their own…

"Technology can be our best friend, and technology can also be the biggest party pooper of our lives. It interrupts our own story, interrupts our ability to have a thought or a daydream, to imagine something wonderful, because we're too busy bridging the walk from the cafeteria back to the office on the cell phone."

STEVEN SPIELBERG.
QUOTE TAKEN FROM 'WHY WE ALL JUST NEED TO PUT DOWN THE PHONE' BY BRIANNA KOLDER IN *THE ODYSSEY ONLINE*, JANUARY 2015.

old skool playlist

- Dig out some old records, tapes, or CDs. Maybe your parents', or maybe some from your own life that you haven't listened to in a decade, or more…

- Choose one – the cheesier, or more obscure, the better…

- Tell whoever's with you why you bought it, and when…

- Maybe even throw some serious shapes to prove how much you loved it, and maybe remember that you still do…

- If you've got access to a record player, why not have a little extra fun playing whatever records you've got at various speeds while you, and whoever you're with, dance around…

- Slow down your dancing when the record is being played slower…

- Speed it up when it's not…

rumble in the jumble

We've all got secrets, things we're ashamed of, aspects of our pasts we'd rather never saw the light of day.

But the game's up – or rather, it's on – because it's time to dig out all those ancient fashion crimes that have been haunting the backs of our wardrobes.

It's time to dig them out and put on a fashion show of your own.

And then, if you're feeling truly inspired, and there's a suitable bar or club nearby – maybe head out to introduce your new look to the world.

play mob

Mob is the perfect game to play anywhere outside. The more 'cover', meaning trees, bushes, parked cars, walls, etc, the better... This is a game of stealth. It's all about adapting to your environment to conceal your movements – so you can win!

The more players, the better.

- First up, you need to choose someone to be **It**.

- Now choose a **Mob Base**. This can be a tree, a drainpipe on a wall, or even a park bench – basically, something that can't be moved.

- Get **It** to close their eyes and face the **Mob Base** and count to a hundred.

- During which time, everyone else playing goes and hides.

'It'

- **It** now has to leave the **Mob Base** they're guarding to see if they can see where the other players are hiding.

- The second they do, they have to a) run back to the **Mob Base** and touch it before the other player reaches it and b) shout, 'Mob, mob, you're out' and then name the player's name. That player is then out.

- The other players have to sneak up and touch the **Mob Base** without being spotted. If even one succeeds, then **It** has to be **It** again.

- And don't forget to try using mass rush tactics ('Mobbing') – where so many players rush the **Mob Base** at the same time that **It** doesn't get a chance to name them all.

time to tweet

Birds are busy in the garden all year round, but in autumn they're off on long-haul flights, or arriving from foreign climes.

Give them a hand with some much-needed fuel.

You can make simple bird feeders out of almost anything.

Thread cereal and blueberries onto a piece of string and hang it on a branch…

Use plastic bottles with a feeding hole cut into the side…

Or even a cup and saucer – anything that delivers seeds, grains, fruit, and rice…

And don't forget to leave out some water, too.

5
ways to be
instantly happier

1. Listening to a favourite piece
of music

2. Spending five more minutes with
someone you like

3. Going outdoors

4. Helping someone else

5. Having a new experience

According to Professor Paul Dolan of the London School of
Economics and Political Science and author of *Happiness by Design*.
Quote taken from 'Five things you can do to be happier right now' by
Sarah Knapton in *The Telegraph*, May 2015.

banana splits

Here's a great trick to play on anyone you know who likes bananas.

🌙 Take a fairly ripe banana and stick in a pin through one of its seams, making a small hole. Don't push the pin out the other side.

🌙 Now move the pin back and forth inside the banana keeping the top very still, so that you're slicing the banana inside the skin, but not tearing or marking the skin itself.

🌙 Repeat in several places, but not on the same side or in a row, or it'll be visible.

🌙 Offer the banana to your friend and watch them peel it.

Enjoy their reaction as it falls apart in their hands.

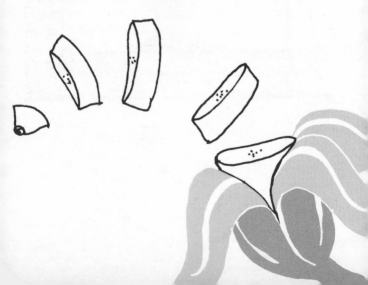

who's who

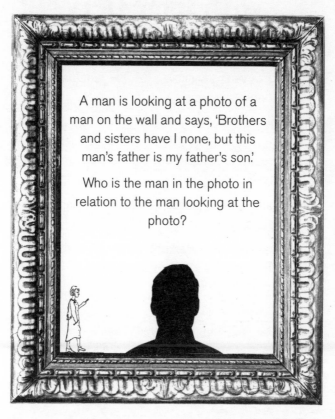

A man is looking at a photo of a man on the wall and says, 'Brothers and sisters have I none, but this man's father is my father's son.'

Who is the man in the photo in relation to the man looking at the photo?

The man in the photo is his son. Why? Because he doesn't have any brothers and sisters, meaning his statement 'my father's son' can only be a reference to himself.

spice up your life with some fiery chilli oil

Some like it hot, but others like it hot, hot, hot! For the latter, chilli oil is a nectar sent straight from the gastronomic gods.

You can use it to add a kick to salads, barbecues, curries, stews, grilled meat or fish. You can drizzle it on corn on the cob, or splash it on cheese on toast.

There are currently nearly 3,000 different varieties of chilli to sample and enjoy, the hottest being the 'Carolina Reaper', grown by the PuckerButt Pepper Company (USA), which rates at a tongue-blistering 1,569,300 Scoville Heat Units (SHU).

More commonly used varieties for cooking include the bird's-eye, Jalapeño, chipotle and Habañero, which you'll find available in most good supermarkets.

To make chilli oil:

- find a variety of chilli you really enjoy, or a few different varieties

- dry them near a radiator or in an airing cupboard

- crumble, flake or grind them into a dry pan and heat for one minute

- cover them with olive oil, stir, and then bottle

- shake the bottle occasionally while in storage to keep the flavours infusing

- Come up with a suitably butt-kicking name for your new creation

WARNING: Always wash hands thoroughly after handling chillies. Avoid contact with the eyes and sensitive skin.

cool down with a 60 second ice cream!

Who doesn't like to chill out with an ice cream beside the seaside on a hot summer's day? But homemade ice cream can make any tea time special, no matter what time of year.

Even better, when you're in charge of the ingredients, as well as making it tasty, you can even make it healthy too.

But best of all is you can make your own ice cream in less than a minute. And here's how.

What you'll need:

→ a hand blender, or food processor

→ low fat yoghurt

→ chopped fruit – strawberries, raspberries, banana, orange, pineapple (tinned or fresh, whichever you prefer)

→ runny honey, or jam

How to make it:

⏱ Freeze the fruit mix

⏱ Mix equal quantities of frozen fruit and yoghurt either with a hand blender or food processor

⏱ Add some honey or jam (or both) to sweeten the mix

⏱ Whiz it to the consistency of smooth ice cream

⏱ Eat it – in a bowl, or a cone

⏱ Make sure to make lots, so you can put some back in the freezer for another day

become a poet or spoken word artist

Read and listen to poetry and spoken word recordings whenever you get the chance. Go to recitals and gigs too if you can.

Write about subjects that interest you and that you know a bit about.

Write from the heart. Don't hold back. Don't be afraid of what others might think. Let your true thoughts and feelings flood out.

If you get stuck, don't worry. Go for a walk, or a shower, or a doze on the sofa to refresh your imagination.

Read your poetry out loud. In secret. Or to your friends. Or even to strangers on a beach.

Don't be afraid to start writing. In fact, why not start now?

Try writing the first few lines of your new poem here

_____

_____

_____

_____

_____

send a postcard

Everything today is instant. Especially the way we communicate.

Take some time out now to write a postcard to someone you love and send it in the post.

See if they write back.

Practise what you're going to say below...

playlist

We're all so used to instant gratification, to radio-friendly, download-friendly three-minute songs.

But how about taking time out to listen to something a bit longer? Switch off the rest of the world and let the music carry you away.

Here's a playlist of longer pieces of music that are quirky, tell a story, or are just plain beautiful…

5 mins	Claude Debussy – Clair De Lune
6.5 mins	Elbow – One Day Like This
9.5 mins	Gustav Mahler – Adagietto from Symphony no. 5
10 mins	Herbie Hancock – Sly
14 mins	Lynyrd Syknryd – Free Bird
26 mins	Pink Floyd - Shine On You Crazy Diamond
1 hr, 4 mins	Sparks – The Seduction of Ingmar Bergman

Or, if you've got a bit – OK, well a lot – more time on your hands, here's the long player to beat them all…

16 hours	Wagner – The Ring Cycle

the fruit factor

There's always been a great tradition of fruit and veg appearing in band names, such as Black Eyed Peas, Red Hot Chili Peppers, Bananarama, The Lemonheads, Smashing Pumpkins & Tangerine Dream, to name but a few…

Well, here's your chance to create your own fruit-tastic group.

What you'll need: **cloves, fruit, veg, imagination**

Now get decorating. They'll need features and personality a-plenty if they're going to succeed in the cut and thrust world of pop.

Here's some we did earlier to get you in the mood…

hippie-fy me!

Instead of buying new clothes, why not add a little Woodstock to your wardrobe this summer by tie-dying some of the threads you've already got?

- First off, head to a craft shop and get some fibre reactive dyes and soda ash.

- Next, soak an old shirt or T-shirt overnight in warm water with soda ash and a pinch of salt (or bicarbonate of soda works too).

- Now, crank up some Janis Joplin or Grateful Dead on the stereo.

- Wring out the shirt and smooth it out on a covered work surface.

- Don your rubber gloves.

- Put a rod, or stick (or your finger will do) in the middle of the fabric and twist until the fabric makes a swirly shape.

- Fix the swirly bundle in place with rubber bands.

- Dip your bunched up shirt in your pot of dye. Or you can use the dye in bottles to colour different sections for more of a rainbow effect.

- Put your masterpiece in a re-sealable plastic bag and leave overnight – preferably during a full moon for extra cosmic love.

- Wash it in cold water until the water runs clear.

- Dry your shirt in the sunshine, before heading for your nearest festival with some flowers in your hair and a smile on your face.

jean genie

Just because your favourite jeans are looking a little worse for wear, doesn't mean you have to throw them out.

Like wine, denim fabric is one of those wonderful things in life that gets better as it ages.

So here are some great ways to up-cycle your much-loved jeans and give them a new lease of life:

Cut them off and make them into shorts – with turn ups or frayed edges

Turn them into a funky handbag

Make new backs for your director's chair

Chop them up into a patchwork quilt

Refashion them into a funky cushion

Cover a photo album with them

Recycle them into place mats for a table

Transform them into aprons, or baby bibs

Use them to patch up a much-loved kids' toy

Convert the pockets into drinks coasters

chillaxify
your soul

meditation is a great way to a clearer, calmer mind, and the relaxation response can be achieved by quietly sitting for 15 minutes a day

anyone can do it

○ sit comfortably – cross legged on the floor or in a chair

○ shut your eyes and concentrate on your breathing

○ really focus on your breath going in and out of your nostrils

○ your head will be full of thoughts to begin with. But the longer you focus on your breathing, the more you'll find you're able to silence this internal chatter

○ let tension go with each exhalation

○ choose a 'guided image', such as a soothing light, or relaxing waterfall, and imagine it washing away tension from your body and mind

○ or choose a mantra, such as 'Om', and mentally repeat it to help you focus

with practice, you'll feel a sense of inner peace and relaxation

let your mind go

Om

lip sync!

It's time to test your pop knowledge – in silence!

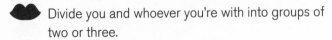 Divide you and whoever you're with into groups of two or three.

Give each group a piece of paper with the name of a famous band and a song on it.

Each group then gets five minutes to practise in a room out of sight and earshot.

They then have to come back and perform the song, but lip syncing it rather than out loud.

Points and prizes for the best and funniest performances.

babyface/ ghostface

The best party games are either silly, or messy. This one's both.

Fill a bowl or saucepan with flour.

Cover it with a plate and then flip it upside down.

Carefully remove the bowl, so that you're left with a mound of flour.

Very gently, place a jelly baby on the top of the mound.

Take turns with your friends to cut a slice from the mound without moving the jelly baby.

Whoever makes the flour collapse has to pick up the jelly baby – using only their mouth.

Make sure to have a camera close at hand to capture this moment – because as whoever loses emerges blinking and encrusted in flour, you'll notice they look about 900 years old and spooky as heck.

boy (moth) meets girl (moth)

How can male moths be attracted? It's a question many moth-watchers, and indeed female moths, have been asking for years.

Some say it's a good sense of humour that attracts them the most. But scientists insist it's everything to do with pheromones instead.

Meaning the best way to lure male moths is with female moths. And the best way to catch female moths… is with food.

Go outside after dark in the spring, summer, or autumn.

Essentials to take with you: a saucer, a mix of sugar and water (to simulate nectar), a cardboard shoebox, a perforated lid or screen lid, an outdoor light or torch.

What to do next:

- 🦋 put the box near the light source with the saucer inside it and pour some liquid onto the saucer

- 🦋 once moths begin feeding on the liquid, gently remove the saucer, closing the moths in with the lid

- 🦋 watch and wait

More moths will keep landing on the lid. But what makes them stay? It's not the food, because it's gone. It's the pheromones being secreted by the female moths inside, which male moths can incredibly smell from up to seven miles away.

Don't forget to set the moths free at the end of your experiment, but perhaps first try identifying a few of them. There are tens of thousands of species to choose from.

rock 'n' roll

We can hunt down pictures online of any creature on the planet at the tap of a keyboard, but there are plenty you can easily hunt down and examine up close in real life too.

Take insects, for example. Here in the UK, there are over 20,000 different kinds – and some of them live a lot nearer than you think.

So let's go hunt some down.

If you can, get hold of a magnifying glass and a book on identifying insects, but if you can't, don't worry, this will still be fun.

Head out into your garden or a nearby park or wood or field.

Lots of insects like living in moist, dark places. One environment that's perfect for them is the soil beneath rocks.

Find a rock that looks like it's not been disturbed for some time. Slowly, carefully turn it over.

Try and identify the insects that you find. Observe how they react to the light. Do they try and run away? Watch where they go next.

Insects to look out for: beetles, earwigs, worms, spiders, millipedes, centipedes, slugs, ants and caterpillars.

Maybe try drawing the one you find most interesting
here

If you go back, you'll notice that the insects you see
under the same rock will vary depending on the time
of year. Try to think of reasons for why this might be.
Check in a book to see if you're right.

Remember: whenever you're finished looking at
insects, always gently put the rock back how you
found it. This is their home, after all.

strawball!

Forget computer football games and forget the World Cup too, the only penalty shootout that counts starts here!

What you'll need: 4 coins, 2 straws, 1 table tennis ball.

Use coins to mark two goals on your kitchen table, or even on the floor.

Take a straw each, then roll the ball into the middle of the pitch.

Use your straws to blow the table tennis ball into your opponent's goal.

FA rules apply.

Keep score

0-5 It's back to the training academy for you.

6-10 Real Madrid ain't coming knocking any time soon.

11-16 Watch out, Ronaldo. There's a new kid on the block.

17-20 The Ballon d'Or is yours!

find stories in a graveyard

That's right, it really is time to meet the ancestors, but in a good way.

Graveyards are beautiful places and, what's more, they're free to look round.

Take some time – while you still can! – to wander around an old graveyard and find some interesting graves and read what's written there.

Make up stories about the people you read about.

Maybe even try and find out more about the real people they were when you get back home.

make a paper movie!

Not to be outdone by other electronic smartphones, your Paper Smartphone has a home movie app too.

To launch it, all you've got to do is grip your Paper Smartphone in the palm of your hand and use your thumb to flick rapidly through the pages, bringing the images on the bottom corners to life.

If you like what you see, why not buy a pad and try making your own film?

To give you an idea of how important it is to only move the story on one frame at a time, here are some 'stills' taken from your Paper Smartphone's movie.

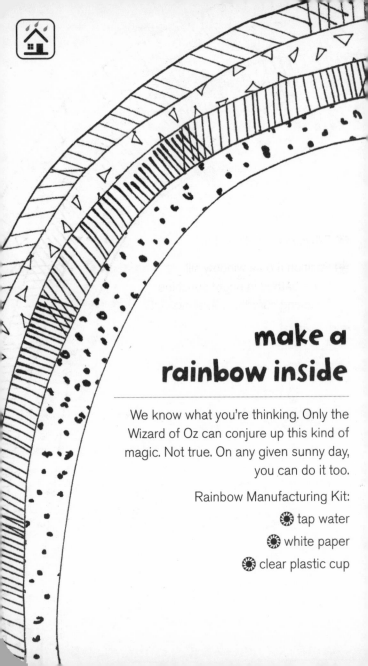

make a
rainbow inside

We know what you're thinking. Only the
Wizard of Oz can conjure up this kind of
magic. Not true. On any given sunny day,
you can do it too.

Rainbow Manufacturing Kit:

- ☀ tap water
- ☀ white paper
- ☀ clear plastic cup

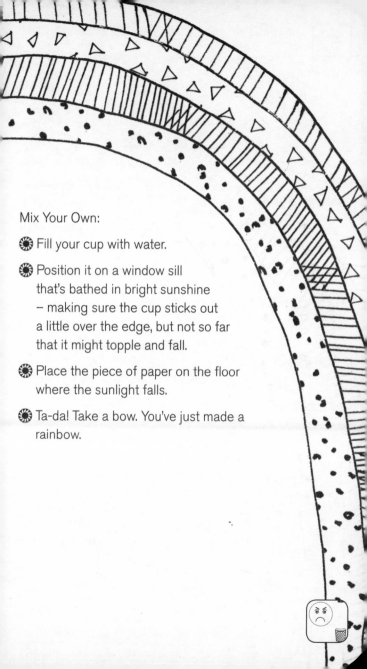

Mix Your Own:

☀ Fill your cup with water.

☀ Position it on a window sill
that's bathed in bright sunshine
– making sure the cup sticks out
a little over the edge, but not so far
that it might topple and fall.

☀ Place the piece of paper on the floor
where the sunlight falls.

☀ Ta-da! Take a bow. You've just made a
rainbow.

fizz buzz!

Fizz Buzz is a deeply difficult, confusing and compelling counting game.

But luckily, whilst extremely hard to do, it's extremely easy to explain.

The goal is to count from one to a hundred out loud.

But – and here's the catch – instead of 3, or multiples of 3, the player must say '**Fizz**'.

And – as if one catch wasn't enough – instead of 5, or multiples of 5, the player must say '**Buzz**'.

Oh… and for any multiples of 3 and 5, you have to say '**Fizz Buzz**'.

As in… 1, 2, Fizz, 4, Buzz, Fizz, 7, 8, Fizz, Buzz, 11, Fizz, 12, 14, Fizz Buzz, etc.

Sounds easy? It's not. Try it. See how far you can get.

Now get a friend to try.

Or even take turns with two people or more in a round, saying a number each, and see if together you can do better.

To make it easier for you to judge how well someone else is doing, here's the sequence in full:

1, 2, Fizz, 4, Buzz, Fizz, 7, 8, Fizz, Buzz, 11, Fizz, 13, 14, Fizz Buzz, 16, 17, Fizz, 19, Buzz, Fizz, 22, 23, Fizz, Buzz, 26, Fizz, 28, 29, Fizz Buzz, 31, 32, Fizz, 34, Buzz, Fizz, 37, 38, 39, Buzz, 41, Fizz, 43, 44, Fizz Buzz, 46, 47, Fizz, 49, Buzz, Fizz, 52, 53, Fizz, Buzz, 56, Fizz, 58, 59, Fizz Buzz, 61, 62, Fizz, 64, Buzz, Fizz, 67, 68, Fizz, Buzz, 71, Fizz, 73, 74, Fizz Buzz, 76, 77, Fizz, 79, Buzz, Fizz, 82, 83, Fizz, Buzz, 86, Fizz, 88, 89, Fizz Buzz, 91, 92, Fizz, 94, Buzz, Fizz, 97, 98, Fizz, Buzz.

surf
(with your whole body, not just your fingertips)

Forget just surfing the world wide web. There's a deep blue sea out there just waiting to be tamed.

You'll need: A surfboard, a wetsuit, suncream, a beach and the sea. And if you have sensitive feet, wet shoes you can wear in the water. A sense of humour and a lack of pride also come in handy for the beginner.

Practise the 'pop up'. You can do this on the beach. Lie your board down and get down yourself. Grip the board's sides, do a push up and 'pop' up your legs under you so that your feet are the board. Now crouch down low, your arms out for support.

Got that?

OK, it's time to get wet. Take your board and wade out into the water, then lie on your belly on the board, and paddle out using a crawl stroke to where the waves are swelling, but not breaking.

Position your board with its nose
towards the beach.

When a good wave comes, paddle like
crazy so you're going the same speed as
the wave and are positioned just before it.

Stay lying down the first few times you catch a
wave and ride it in.

Then try to 'pop up' on your board, and crouch with
your hands out for balance.

Practice riding waves home over and over, adjusting
your position each time. You'll nose dive if you're too far
forward. The wave will leave you behind if you're too far
back.

Simple. Now all you've got to do is learn to do this
standing up. Oh, and maybe ride a hundred foot tube
wave – whilst whistling your favourite Beach Boys tune.

gunfight
at the h2o corral

1. **Weapons** – if you've got plastic pistols or blasters that you've bought in a shop, then good for you. But this doesn't mean you're going to win. Anything goes in a water fight, so long as it can hold water and be used to drench your enemies like the drowned rats they truly are. We're talking – saucepans, washing up liquid bottles, spray bottles, buckets, your bare hands, the garden hose, and don't forget you're going to need water bombs and balloons as grenades.

2. **Ammunition** – by which, of course, we mean water. Make sure you've got plenty of it around. A paddling pool, or a nearby sink, should do the trick.

3. **Neutral zones** – decide where you can and cannot go during the ensuing conflict. Probable no-go areas will include much of the indoors of any family home.

4. **Fight in teams** – and take no prisoners. 'The Wetter, the Better' is the only motto you'll need.

Variations:

Play 'Water Tag', where the second you get shot, you're 'It'.

Duel. Stand back to back and walk ten paces, then spin round and fire. The first to score a hit is the winner.

Trivia! The world's biggest water fight takes place during the Songkran Festival in Thailand each year, with many of the country's 60 million inhabitants getting involved. Ice trucks even patrol the streets for refueling!

navigate by leaf!

Stuck in the wild? Lost your compass? In imminent danger of being chased by a bear? Yeah, we've all been there, but next time you're in deep despair and don't know which way to turn, fear not. Here's a simple way to get you safely back home.

A compass is an instrument that detects the earth's magnetic field. It finds which way is north and then which way all other directions are too.

N

E

Bare Necessities Needed to Make a Compass in the Wild

- a pin or a needle
- a small leaf
- water
- a magnet (or, if you don't have one on you, you can still magnetise a needle with a steel or iron nail, silk or fur, or even your own hair)

Magnetise your needle – either by rubbing it with a magnet back and forth 50 times, or by doing the same with silk, fur, or hair. Or, if you're using a steel or iron nail, just stick the needle into a piece of wood, then use the nail to tap it 50 times.

Find some still water (a cupful, or a puddle) and place your leaf gently on the surface, keeping the topside dry.

Put the needle gently lengthways on the leaf. The magnetized needle will align with the natural magnetic field of the earth, pointing the leaf along the magnetic north-south axis.

Now look around and see which way the shadows are pointing (they'll point west at dawn, north at midday, and east at dusk). Whichever end of the needle is pointing closest to the shadows' direction will be north.

Now align your map, if you have one, so its north is pointing north too. Then choose a reference point on the horizon and head for home.

LAPTOP™

....

For Him & Her!
LapTop™ **brings**
you closer
together!

NIGHT OWL

Perfect at
bedtime too!

*Laptop™ is compatible with both **ChatRoom™**, **Hand™** and **Smile™**, but using in tandem with **Glovelok™** is liable to cause it to crash.

could it be magic?

Try placing a needle onto the surface of a glass of water and guess what? It sinks.

But there's a way to stop this happening and the secret is to stop water getting into the eye of the needle.

There are two ways you can do this.

First way:

Place a strip of tissue paper on the water's surface and then gently drop the needle on top. The tissue will become soaked and will sink – but the needle will stay floating.

Second way:

Position the needle across the prongs of a fork and very slowly lower the fork into the water, watching the needle carefully and keeping it flat to prevent water from getting into its eye. Once the fork is fully submerged, carefully pull it away, leaving the needle floating on the surface of the water.

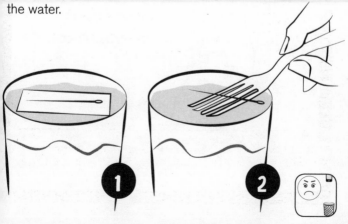

ice magic

Ever wondered how to pick up an ice cube with just a piece of string or cotton? Go on, admit it. Of course you have. Because think of all the amazing things you then could do, like, er, play ice conkers, or, er, swing it back and forth and try and hypnotise yourself.

OK, so there aren't actually that many really good practical applications for this trick, but it's still pretty neat.

Essential equipment:

 an ice cube

 an 8 inch (20 cm) piece of string or cotton

salt

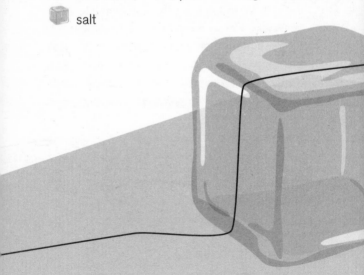

Performing the trick:

Step 1 – Put the cube on a flat surface such as a table

Step 2 – Lie the string flat across it, so it dangles down over either end

Step 3 – Sprinkle some salt over the area where the string and cube meet

Step 4 – Wait three to four minutes

Step 5 – Hold either end of the string and gently lift it – the cube should lift up too

So how does this happen? Well, it's magic, of course. But OK, so there's a bit of science too. Salt makes the ice melt by dropping its melting point. This lets the string form a groove in the ice. The water then refreezes, locking the string in, and making the cube easy to lift.

killer app

Every phone has to have a killer app.

Well, here's ours.

- Get some friends together.

- Rip up some pieces of paper to match the number of players.

- Write 'murderer' on one piece of paper.

- Write 'detective' on another.

- Leave all the other pieces blank.

- Screw up the pieces of paper and put them into a hat or bowl.

- Players choose a piece each and secretly open them.

- The detective declares who he/she is, but the murderer keeps quiet.

- Switch off the lights.

- The murderer can move around and touch the victim, who then lies down. The murderer then moves away, but everyone else stays put.

- As the lights come on, the detective now gets to question everyone.

- The murderer lies, but everyone else has to tell the truth.

- By asking questions and examining where the 'body' fell, the detective should be able to deduce who the killer is.

- The detective gets two guesses, or the murderer gets away with it.

The door

Go and open the door.
  Maybe outside there's
  a tree, or a wood,
  a garden,
  or a magic city

Go and open the door.
  Maybe a dog's rummaging.
  Maybe you'll see a face,
or an eye,
or the picture
            of a picture.

Go and open the door.
  If there's a fog
  it will clear.

Go and open the door.
  Even if there's only
  the darkness ticking,
  even if there's only
  the hollow wind,
  even if
            nothing
                    is there,
go and open the door.

At least
there'll be
a draught.

MIROSLAV HOLUB

Translated from the Czech by Ian Milner.
Taken from *Poems Before & After* by Miroslav Holub.

marshmallow heights

Every architect has to start somewhere, but for most people, getting their first building off the ground is no easy matter. There's land to find, planning permission to consider, a workforce to gather.

For your first attempt, you're probably better off scaling things down.

For your steel girders: use toothpicks.

For the cement, nuts and bolts required to secure your girders in place: use mini-marshmallows, of course.

The aim is to build the best building the fastest – but be warned, not all those marshmallows will hold.

A building will only be deemed a success and fit for use if it stays standing following its completion for a full ten seconds.

You can design your own.

Or replicate a classic.

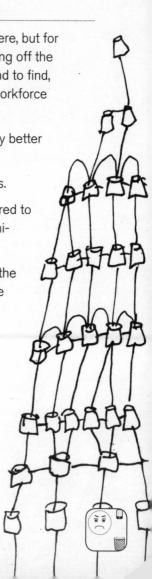

skim it!

First up find a decent expanse of water – such as a lake, a pond, a calm river or the sea.

A lot of these, as luck would have it, come 'supplied' with plenty of stones around them – almost as if they were in some way designed with stone skimming in mind.

Find yourself some decent stones. The rounder and flatter these are, the better, though it's possible to skim most stones that have even a single flat side.

Try and find stones that are roughly the same size as your palm, so they'll be easy for you to throw.

Once you're armed with a few, get up nice and close to the water's edge.

Turn sideways to the water, your arm down low.

With a flick of your wrist, spin the rock at a 20 degree angle toward the water. Watch it bounce, or 'skim' off the water and fly through the air, before skimming off the water again.

If it doesn't bounce and instead just sinks, then adjust your angle next time and look for smoother stones.

Trivia! The Guinness World Record holder for stone skimming is Kurt Steiner. He scored 88 consecutive skips of a stone on water in September 2013 in Pennsylvania, USA.

Your job, of course, is to beat him, and make that record your own.

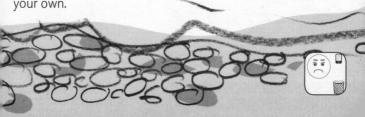

card sharp

Anyone can blow a business card over, right?

Wrong.

Get a business card and fold over its edges as shown below, then stand it on a table.

Now turn it to face someone you know, and position it nice and close to them, and challenge them to blow it over.

They might huff and they might puff, but try as they might, they won't be able to do it – all they'll make it do is slide.

Unless – and here's the trick – they step back and stand about two feet from the table and then lightly blow, directing their breath just slightly in front of the card.

That's it… softly, softly does it… and watch it flip.

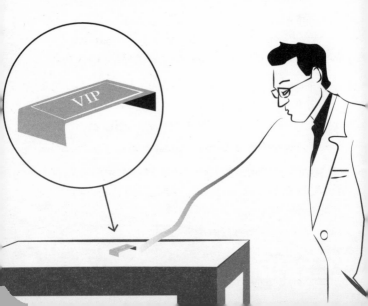

shiver me timbers

As anyone with a drop of pirate's blood in their body will already know, a treasure map is the starting point of any swashbuckling adventure. So why not make your own map?

First decide what you want to hide and where. Then stealthily hide your treasure.

Now gather up some paper, pens, tea bags and a ribbon.

Rip the edges off the paper, or even singe them, so that you have an authentically dog-eared looking map shape.

Dip the teabags in water and then rub them over the paper, letting the brown liquid soak in. Coffee works too.

Put the paper somewhere to dry — an airing cupboard, or on a very low heat in the oven for five minutes.

Now draw on your treasure map, adding in landmarks.

And remember of course, that X marks the spot.

DON'T FORGET! September 19th is officially Talk Like a Pirate Day, the perfect day for a Pirate Party and a treasure hunt for you and your murderous crew.

7 reasons to sleep alone

According to Ofcom, 8 out of 10 people in the UK sleep with their phones next to the bed. It's no wonder we've become a nation of insomniacs.

Here are 7 reasons to kick your phones out of the bedroom now:

1. Studies have shown that the powerful blue light given off by phones inhibits the release of melatonin, the hormone responsible for getting us off to sleep

2. The light of a normal cell phone also stimulates the cells in the retina, which transmit messages to the brain telling it what time of day it is. We trick our brain into thinking it's daytime, when we should be going to sleep

3. The way we use phones – holding them close to our faces – stimulates the brain even more, making us very alert just before sleeping. Experts say that we need at least an hour away from a screen late at night in order to get a good night's sleep

4. Humans are designed to sleep in 1½ hour to 2 hour cycles during the night with very brief moments when we partially wake up in between. This stems from our ancient ancestors, who had to stay alert to predators. We hardly notice these waking moments, but if we get any stimulation during them, such as a vibration from a text message, or even the briefest flash of light, we become alert

5. If we know there's a text or update in the night, such is our level of phone addiction, we can't help ourselves looking at it, which immediately stimulates the cognitive parts of the brain, making it much more difficult to go back to sleep

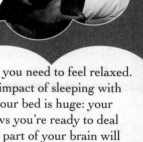

6. In order to sleep, you need to feel relaxed. The psychological impact of sleeping with a phone next to your bed is huge: your subconscious knows you're ready to deal with problems and part of your brain will stay alert, waiting for a phone signal. It's very psychologically stressful to feel that you have to be available 24/7

7. Your mobile phone 'talks' constantly to a base station using radio waves – a type of electromagnetic radiation which research has shown may affect electrical activity in the brain during sleep

freak out!

Being scared should feel, well, scary. And it does. But weirdly, at the same time, scaring yourself stupid can be a lot of fun as well.

One of the best ways to achieve this is to make up a ghost story. Obviously, this will work better at night, or somewhere really spooky.

So gather your friends around in a circle. Turn the lights down low.

Have one of you start out as the narrator. Their job is to set the scene and make the start of the story full of devilish possibilities.

Then, just when the narrator gets to a really good cliffhanger, have them stop, and let the person next to them take over the telling of the tale.

How long can you make the story last?
How scary can you make it?

Does anyone know any other good ghost stories?

And what was that creaking, hissing, *growling* noise you just heard over there?

concentrate!

This is a fun clapping game to test your memory and your nerve. Two players make a clapping rhythm, doing an up/down clap, a hands together high-five style clap and then three single claps on their own.

One player chooses a subject after the first rhyme and then the other player has to name something in that category. So, if it was, say, animals, the person going first could say, elephant. The second player now has to name another animal on the next up clap, and then it swaps to the other player and so on.

CHANT:

This is a game of concentration,
No repeats, or hesitation,
I'll go first,
And you'll go second,
The subject is...

Subjects can be simple: animals, colours, countries, boys' or girls' names, parts of the body, food you find in a fridge.

It works best if the hand clapping speeds up with each round, with three frenetic claps in between to give the players time to think.

You'll be surprised how easy it is for the mind to go completely blank under pressure.

"Don't keep forever on the public road, going only where others have gone. Leave the beaten track occasionally and dive into the woods. You will be certain to find something you have never seen before. Of course it will be a little thing, but do not ignore it. Follow it up, explore around it; one discovery will lead to another, and before you know it you will have something worth thinking about to occupy your mind. All really big discoveries are the result of thought."

Alexander Graham Bell,
inventor of the telephone

missions impossible

We all think we know our limitations, what we can do and what we can't.

Stand with your back to a wall, and keep your heels, hips and shoulders pressed up against it.

Now… without leaning forward, try and jump.

Sit down on an armless, straight-backed chair, with your feet flat on the floor, your back against the chair back and your arms folded across your chest.

Now… try and stand up.

Stand sideways to a wall, keeping your right foot and your cheek pressed up against it.

Now… try and lift your left foot.

perky piñata

Making your own piñata covers all the bases of fun: lots of messy papier mâché, balloon popping and sweets – what's not to love?

Let's get to it.

1. Design your piñata shape. It's best if you model the 'body' of your shape or animal on a balloon as this will form the cavity for the sweets.

2. Cover your work surface and put on an apron or old clothes. This is the messy part.

3. Make your papier mâché balloon paste by mixing 2 cups of flour with 2 cups of water and a tablespoon of salt.

4. Cut or rip up newspaper into strips.

5. Blow up a large balloon. As big as it'll go.

6. If you want to make an animal shape, now's the time to add bits onto the balloon. Carefully tape on arms, legs, snouts, etc, using cardboard boxes or the inners of toilet or kitchen rolls.

7. Soak strips of newspaper in your paste one at a time and lay them over the entire structure. Do several layers. NB: Remember to leave the knot of the balloon exposed so you can pop it.

8. Leave to dry.

9. Now it's time to decorate it with paint and strips of coloured crepe paper.

10. Cut the exposed knot off the balloon and remove it from inside the piñata. Cut away the edges if you need to make the hole bigger.

11. Put two holes around the main hole and feed through wire or ribbon on one side and knot it. Then feed through the other side and knot to make a hanging hook.

12. Fill with sweets. Nothing too big and preferably wrapped, as they'll be falling on the floor.

13. Hang up your piñata. Inside or out is fine, but make sure there's room around it.

14. Now, taking it in turns with your family or friends, whack the piñata with a stick or a broom handle until the papier mâché breaks apart and the sweets fall out.

strum it

Crazy, but true – you only need to learn 3 simple chords on the guitar to start down the road to rock stardom.

All you need to do is master G, C and D and, before you can say 'Take me to Memphis', you'll be playing 12 bar blues and a whole range of classics, including 'I'm a Believer', 'Sweet Home Alabama', 'Knocking on Heaven's Door' and 'You Can't Always Get What You Want'.

These guitar tabs show a guitar neck as if you're looking at an upright guitar.

The numbers represent which finger you put on which string and where. The horizontal lines show the frets, or metal bits under the string.

An X above a string means don't play it. An O means play it, but with no fingers pressing down on it.

There. That's all there is to it. So get strumming.

And, once you've mastered the chords, master a few songs too.

To get you started, here's the chord sequence for Johnny Cash's 'Ring of Fire':

GCG

GCG

CG

DG

DCG

D

CG

DG

G Major

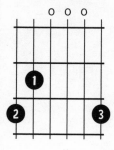

C Major

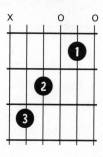

D Major

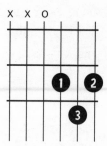

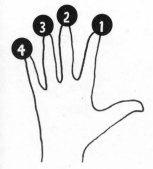

Evan Williams, a founder of Blogger, Twitter and Medium, and his wife, Sara Williams, said that in lieu of iPads, their two young boys have hundreds of books (yes, physical ones) that they can pick up and read anytime

From 'Steve Jobs Was a Low-Tech Parent' by Nick Bilton, *The New York Times*, September 2014.

holy moley!

This Paper Smartphone is so advanced
it can read your mind.

But that's impossible, you say.

Fine, try this.

Think of a number – any number – between 1 and 10.

Double it.

Add 6.

Divide by 2.

Subtract the original number you thought of.

Carefully rip through this hole here to see the number
you're thinking of now.

WARNING! THIS
AREA IS UNSTABLE!
HOLES LIABLE TO
APPEAR

trials of hercules

So you think you're tough? Yeah, really, you do?
Well, OK. Let's find out.

1

Can you blow
up a balloon inside
a bottle?

2

Can you fold a piece of
paper in half more than
nine times?

3

Can you place a matchstick across the
back of your middle finger and under the
first and third fingers at the joints nearest
the fingertips – and then break it?

Answer to all three: no, you can't. Because all three tasks are –
surprise, surprise – impossible.

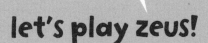

let's play zeus!

Lightning is electricity that jumps within a cloud, or between a cloud and the ground.

The average temperature of lightning is 54,000 degrees Fahrenheit — five times hotter than the surface of the sun.

Lightning flashes 3 million times each day around the world.

Thousands of people are struck by lightning each year.

But possibly the weirdest thing about lightning is that it's possible to make it at home with nothing more complicated than 2 balloons and a woollen glove.

You'll need to inflate both balloons.

Rub one against a smooth wall and the other on the woollen glove.

Draw the curtains and switch out the lights.

Hold a balloon in each hand and slowly, ever-so-slowly, move them closer together, until –

So how did that happen?

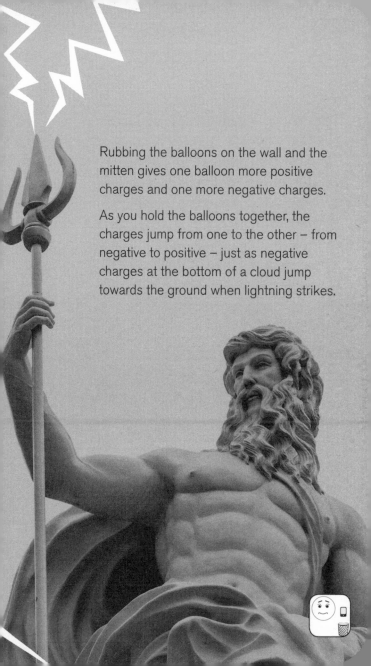

Rubbing the balloons on the wall and the mitten gives one balloon more positive charges and one more negative charges.

As you hold the balloons together, the charges jump from one to the other – from negative to positive – just as negative charges at the bottom of a cloud jump towards the ground when lightning strikes.

I have no idea how to get in touch with anyone anymore. Everyone, it seems, has a home phone, a cell phone, a regular e-mail account, a Facebook account, a Twitter account, and a Web site. Some of them also have a Google Voice number. There are the sentimental few who still have fax machines. If you want to be completely quaint, there are also physical mailing addresses.

Susan Orlean

From 'Communication Fatigue'
by Susan Orlean,
The New Yorker,
May 2011.

spammed™

100 BILLION SPAM EMAILS ARE SENT EACH DAY

8 MILLION SPAM TEXTS ARE SENT IN THE UK EACH DAY

3 MILLION SPAM PHONE CALLS ARE MADE IN THE UK EACH DAY

1 EASY SOLUTION TO IT ALL – Switch It Off!

So why are we all addicted to our phones

Find yourself checking your phone in the middle of the night? First thing in the morning? At the dinner table? You are not alone. Checking your mobile phone IS addictive and here's why.

Dr Susan Weinschenk , an eminent behaviour psychologist and consultant in neuropsychology, and the author of *100 Things Every Designer Needs To Know About People*, says that it's all to do with dopamine loops.

You've heard of dopamine, right? It's created in your brain and is to do with pleasure, but new research has shown that along with feeling pleasure, dopamine makes you seek out pleasure. In short, dopamine makes you curious.

The problem is that you tend to seek out more than you need.

With the internet, tweets and texting, you have almost instant gratification of your desire to seek. Dopamine makes you seek, then you get rewarded for the seeking, which makes you want to seek more. Now you're in a dopamine loop.

The problem is that the dopamine system is never satisfied. There's no 'off' button. It wants more, more, more. So even though you've found the information you wanted, you still seek more. This is why we all click on other links online, even when we have the answer we were looking for.

Dopamine is also stimulated by unpredictability. Emails, texts and tweets show up, but we don't know exactly when. This keeps our dopamine systems stimulated.

Worse, the dopamine system is particularly sensitive to 'cues' that a reward is coming. If there's a small, specific cue that something is going to happen – like a text alert, for example, or a visual clue, it sets off our dopamine system.

The dopamine system is most powerfully stimulated when the information is small enough not to fully satisfy. A short text or a 140 character tweet can set your dopamine system raging.

And it's exhausting – all this dopamine stimulation. The constant switching of attention makes it impossible to concentrate and get anything done.

So, how do you stop a dopamine loop? Switch off all the cues. Change the settings on your phone so you don't get constant notifications.

Or better still – just **switch it off**

time capsule

A time capsule is a collection of objects and information, which is deliberately sealed or buried in the hope future generations will open it up and gain insights about what life was like today.

Just as important, they're great fun to make.

You'll need:

→ a strong, airtight container

→ somewhere to bury it where it won't be disturbed for a while, but where it still might be found one day

time capsule

What to put inside:

→ this really is up to you, although obviously what you can include will be affected by the size of the container

→ you should avoid anything that might decompose, as well as anything containing batteries, or rubber, as they're likely to give off corrosive substances over time

→ wood gives off acid too, especially oak, so make sure to keep it sealed off from any electronic or metal items in the capsule

→ black and white photos should be used rather than colour as they're less likely to fade

→ store documents in separate polyester bags to protect them

Once you're done, make sure to bury your capsule in a cool, dry place.

The International Time Capsule Society keeps a register of all known time capsules. Why not register yours too?

defy gravity!

New does not always equal best. Particularly when it comes to magic.

People have been astonishing each other with the "Light as a Feather" party trick for hundreds of years. It even gets a mention in Samuel Pepys' famous diary in 1665.

There are two parts to the trick, both equally wonderful and weird.

Part 1. Light as a Feather

Place a chair on the floor with plenty of space around it and get your 'victim' to sit on it.

Have four other people, each clasp their hands together and place their forefingers under each corner of the chair's seat.

Now try, but deliberately fail, to lift the victim.

Walk around the victim, chanting, 'Light as a feather, stiff as a board,' for a whole minute.

Then try the lift again and you'll be surprised how easy it now really is.

EXPLANATION: The chanting focuses the lifters' minds, so they lift as a team. It also makes the victim tense up and become easier to lift.

Part 2. Touch the ceiling!

Repeat the steps in Part 1, only this time tell your victim to keep their eyes shut.

Have the lifters make all sorts of noises about how high they're lifting the chair – while in reality only lifting it a few inches off the ground.

Another person now gently presses a book on the head of the victim, while everyone tells them their head is touching the ceiling. They'll believe you too.

really
great britain

Feel like heading out, but you don't know what to do, and you don't know where to go?

Allow us to help with this handy, pocket-sized guide.

11,000 miles of coastland

2,200 miles of canals and rivers

3,000 campsites

300 National Trust Houses and Buildings

200 National Trust Gardens and Parks

120 mountains, or peaks over 600m

68 prehistoric sites

46 Areas Of Outstanding National Beauty

28 Unesco World Heritage Sites

CONSTABLE

First published in Great Britain in 2015 by Constable

Copyright in text © 2015 Josie Lloyd and Emlyn Rees

The moral right of the authors has been asserted.

A CIP catalogue record for this book is available from the
British Library.

ISBN: 978-1-47212-178-3

Page design by D.R. ink

Printed and bound in Great Britain by Clays Ltd.

Papers used by Constable are from well-managed forests and other
responsible sources.

MIX
Paper from
responsible sources
FSC
www.fsc.org   FSC® C104740

Constable
An imprint of
Little, Brown Book Group
Carmelite House
50 Victoria Embankment
London EC4Y 0DZ

An Hachette UK Company
www.hachette.co.uk

www.littlebrown.co.uk

Text Permissions

'The Door' reproduced from *Poems Before & After: Collected English Translations* (Bloodaxe Books, 2006) by permission of
the publisher.

Image Permissions

Front cover, icons: top row far right, second row far right, third row first left, third row second left, last row far left, last three
on the right © Shutterstock

Back cover image © Shutterstock

Tricksy pixiez icon, arty farty icon, dares and challenges icon (as seen throughout), p10, p17 (outline of Dot Com image),
p19, p20 (fish), p22-3 (sun main image and motif), p24 (Nice Slice border), p28, p35, p38, p43, p47, p54, p56, p61 (rose
pattern), p63 (shark), p64, p65, p71, p80-1 (background pattern), p88-9, p91, p92, p99 (wave), p100-1, p106-7, p115, p117,
p120-1 (elephant), p123 (brick wall), p133, p140 © Shutterstock

Edible zombie makeover photograph ©Josie Lloyd & Emlyn Rees

All other illustrations © Emil Dacanay and Sian Rance, D.R. ink